Dear Parents:

Congratulations! Your child is taking the first steps on an exciting journey. The destination? Independent reading!

STEP INTO READING® will help your child get there. The program offers five steps to reading success. Each step includes fun stories and colorful art or photographs. In addition to original fiction and books with favorite characters, there are Step into Reading Non-Fiction Readers, Phonics Readers and Boxed Sets, Sticker Readers, and Comic Readers—a complete literacy program with something to interest every child.

Learning to Read, Step by Step!

Ready to Read   Preschool–Kindergarten
• big type and easy words • rhyme and rhythm • picture clues
For children who know the alphabet and are eager to begin reading.

Reading with Help   Preschool–Grade 1
• basic vocabulary • short sentences • simple stories
For children who recognize familiar words and sound out new words with help.

Reading on Your Own   Grades 1–3
• engaging characters • easy-to-follow plots • popular topics
For children who are ready to read on their own.

Reading Paragraphs   Grades 2–3
• challenging vocabulary • short paragraphs • exciting stories
For newly independent readers who read simple sentences with confidence.

Ready for Chapters   Grades 2–4
• chapters • longer paragraphs • full-color art
For children who want to take the plunge into chapter books but still like colorful pictures.

STEP INTO READING® is designed to give every child a successful reading experience. The grade levels are only guides; children will progress through the steps at their own speed, developing confidence in their reading. The F&P Text Level on the back cover serves as another tool to help you choose the right book for your child.

Remember, a lifetime love of reading starts with a single step!

Copyright © 1990 by Richard Scarry
All rights reserved. This 2015 edition was published in the United States by Random House
Children's Books, a division of Random House LLC, a Penguin Random House Company,
New York. Originally published in a slightly different form by Random House Children's Books,
New York, in 1990.

Visit us on the Web!
StepIntoReading.com
randomhousekids.com

Educators and librarians, for a variety of teaching tools, visit us at
RHTeachersLibrarians.com

Library of Congress Cataloging-in-Publication Data
Scarry, Richard.
Richard Scarry's Be careful, Mr. Frumble!
   pages   cm.
"Originally published in a slightly different form by Random House Children's Books,
New York, in 1990." —Copyright page.
Summary: Mr. Frumble's plan to go for a walk is directed by the wind, which carries his
hat off from one place to another causing many near-disasters.
ISBN 978-0-385-38449-0 (pbk.) — ISBN 978-0-375-97346-8 (lib. bdg.) —
ISBN 978-0-385-38450-6 (ebook)
[1. Hats—Fiction. 2. Winds—Fiction. 3. Animals—Fiction.] I. Title. II. Title: Be careful,
Mr. Frumble!
PZ7.S327Rfh 2015   [E]—dc23   2013035224

Printed in the United States of America
10 9 8 7 6 5 4 3 2 1

This book has been officially leveled by using the F&P Text Level Gradient™ Leveling System.

STEP INTO READING®

3 1526 04649428 9

2

STEP

READING WITH HELP

RICHARD SCARRY'S BUSY WORLD

Richard Scarry's

BE CAREFUL, MR. FRUMBLE!

Random House 🏠 New York

Mr. Frumble
is going
for a walk.

4

He grabs his hat.

The wind is really blowing today!

Hold on to your hat,
Mr. Frumble.

10

Uh-oh!
There goes your hat,
Mr. Frumble!

Do not sell that hat,

Mr. Grocer!

Now where is your hat?

Do not serve that hat,

Mr. Waiter!

The hat blew into
the train.

Stop, train!

Uh-oh!
Those birds are making
a nest in it.
Stop, birds!

Be careful, Mr. Frumble!

Where is your hat?

Oh, dear!

Look where your hat is,

Mr. Frumble!

Be careful,

Mr. Frumble!

Splash!

There is your hat,

Mr. Frumble!

Did you have a nice walk,

Mr. Frumble?

"Why, yes, I did!
Thank you, Hat!"